NEENY COMING, NEENY GOING

BY KAREN ENGLISH · PAINTINGS BY SYNTHIA SAINT JAMES

BridgeWater Books

For all the African-American descendants of the Sea Islands.
    —S.S.J.

To Sea Island children, past and present.
    —K.E.

Library of Congress Cataloging-in-Publication Data
English, Karen.
Neeny coming, Neeny going / by Karen English; pictures
by Synthia Saint James.
p.   cm.
Summary: Essie eagerly awaits the visit of her cousin but
feels disheartened after her arrival because Neeny is no
longer interested in life on the island from which she
moved.
ISBN 0-8167-3796-7
[1. Afro-Americans—Juvenile fiction.   [1. Afro-
Americans—Fiction.   2. Islands—Fiction.   3. Cousins—
Fiction.]   I. Saint James, Synthia, ill.   II. title.
PZ7.E7232Ne   1996   [E]—dc20   95-3624

TO THE READER

Daufuskie Island, where this story is set, has seen many changes. Located off the coast of South Carolina, it was once known for its Sea Island cotton and its oyster beds. It was also the home of a culture that blended American and West African customs. The language, too, was a blend of African and English.

This story is set in the 1950s. By that time, pollution had begun to destroy the oyster beds and the island way of life. Many islanders had to move to the mainland. NEENY COMING, NEENY GOING represents that loss—and the sorrow that often accompanies change.

"Neeny coming—Neeny coming tomorrow!"

"Is that so?" Dada ask, teasing me. Our grandma know Neeny is coming. She smile at me and pull a sheet from her basket and give it a big shake. The wind lift it up and it flutter like the wing of a bird. Dada pin it to the line. Dada's sheets are the whitest on 'Fuskie Island. Everyone say so.

I turn and run to the creek shore where Uncle Dink is mending his crab net. "Neeny coming, Uncle Dink!"

He look up. "Is that so?" he shout back. "It been long time, right?"

I run through the tall grass to meet Grandpa coming up the road
in the oxcart. "Grandpa—Neeny coming! She coming tomorrow!"
   "Yeah, sure, gal. We all know Neeny coming. Get in the wagon
and I take you home."

We pass the schoolhouse where Miss James teach all the children on the island. It summertime and no one there, but I yell at the schoolhouse anyway, "Neeny coming tomorrow!"

I look up at the sky just then and see an osprey nest high up in a tree. "Neeny coming!" I tell that old nest.

I see egrets fishing the shore of the river. "Neeny coming tomorrow!" I yell to them. They keep on fishing.

Me and my cousin, Neeny, live like sisters until Aunt Marie send for her. Then Neeny go far away to live with her mama in the big city on the mainland, and I don't ever see her again.

In the morning the low tide make the air smell strong and salty. Dada say I can go and meet Neeny's boat. I hear the groan of the boat before it put-put into sight. Then I see it round the bend with Neeny sitting behind Uncle Dink, holding a parasol the color of peach blossoms. Ah . . . is that Neeny? I squint my eyes. She seem different. But, no mind—Neeny here!

Before Neeny can get off the boat, I throw my arms around her.
"Neeny here at last!" I'm so happy—my heart dancing!
   "Ah, cousin, don't rock me like that. You make me feel more seasick."
   I grab her small suitcase and balance it on my head. Uncle Dink
carry the big one. Up the road we go.
   "Be careful with my cases now," Neeny say. "Those are brand-new."

"Neeny here!" I shout to Mr. Frogmore behind his mule, plowing his great field.

Mr. Frogmore shout back, "So you back among us, Neeny!"

"Just for a little visit, Mr. Frogmore." She raise her parasol over her head and give it a twirl. I think tomorrow we get up early and pick blackberries after chores so Dada can make a cobbler. Next day we go bogging for crabs in the marsh, next day we collect sweet grass for basketmaking. Oh, I got plans . . .

But next day, when I get up early—Neeny don't. I feed the chickens, rake the front yard and put a pretty swirly pattern in it—for Neeny. Then I sit on the porch and wait . . . and wait . . . and wait. Better to pick blackberries before the sun get too hot, I think. But Neeny don't come out onto the porch until the sun is high.

She stretch, yawn, and flop down next to me. I don't say nothing. I'm a tiny bit mad at her. She know we get up early to pick berries. What wrong with her?

"Too hot to pick berries now," I say.

"Too much trouble anyway," Neeny say, rubbing her eyes.

"And Dada already gone to market—she won't make cobbler now."

"I'm too tired to move off this porch," Neeny say. "I've traveled a long way, Essie. First I take the cab to the bus depot, then I take the bus to the riverboat, then down the river, then Uncle Dink pick me up in the fishing boat . . ." Neeny wipe her forehead with the back of her hand. "I too fatigued."

I picture Neeny traveling. "You do all that?"

"Close your mouth, silly girl. That's nothing. I been on a train before, too."

"Dada won't even let me go across the water," I say. "She too afraid the weather get bad and the boat turn over and I drown."

"That's because she don't know no better."

I look at Neeny. I look at her hard. How can she say that about Dada? Dada know everything.

Next morning Neeny get up earlier. But for what? Nothing! That girl lean against our porch rail and watch me do all the work. She fan herself with a palmetto branch and sweep away flies.

"My mama works for a high-class family in Charleston," she tell me. "They have a gardener to take care of their yard."

I press my lips together and hold my tongue.

Neeny look off toward our pine grove. "They have big trees in their yard. When the weather's nice, Mrs. Forrester—the lady of the house—take her afternoon coffee at a little outdoor table in the shade."

Neeny don't see me when I stick out my tongue at her.

Later, Dada call us inside so she can braid my hair. Neeny watch her fast fingers. Then she say, "My mama sent me to the beauty parlor for my birthday and I got Shirley Temple curls." Dada say nothing, but I feel her thinking. "I got a purple velvet headband and a birthday cake with five pink roses on it and ten pink candles. Mama took me for ice cream, too."

Dada and I look at each other.

I think Neeny talk too much. And all about herself. She don't ask how Dada back trouble is. She don't ask about the big factory that might be messin' up the waters for shrimpin'. Or how'd Uncle Dink like it if he couldn't crab or shrimp no more. Neeny talk about Neeny.

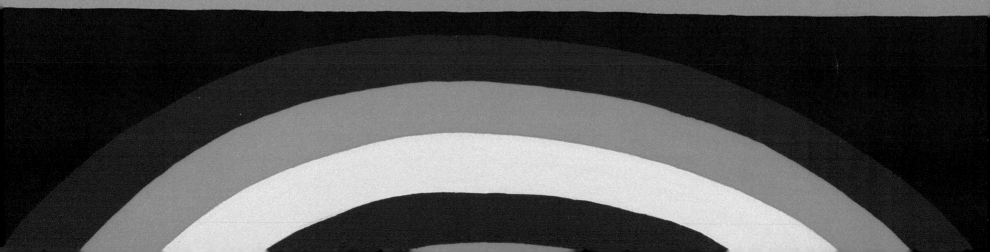

After lunch Dada send us down the road with a basket of yams for Miss Alljoy. Miss Alljoy delivered all the children of the island. Neeny, too. She always have benne candy for us. Before we leave, Miss Alljoy bring out a tray of benne. My mouth water and I take a big piece. Neeny break off a little piece and bite off a tiny corner, then poke around in her mouth with her baby finger. Later she tell me, "I don't like the way the sesame seeds get in my teeth. Chocolate candy's better."

When Uncle Dink and I go bogging for crab, Neeny just watch
from the pier. When I gather sweet grass for Dada's baskets, Neeny
sit on the shore and look out at the water like she want to swim home.

"Okay, Miss Neeny," Dada say after we get back. "Let's see what
you remember."

Neeny's fingers forget what Dada show them. She don't wrap the
palmetto tight around the sweet grass bundle like she should.

"I like embroidery better. Embroidery is what a lady does."

I look at Dada. Dada smile. "Is that so," she say. "Well, you fine
ladies—you got the wash to hang up. Now run and get to it."

"Look at this, Neeny," I say, pulling my new bed quilt out of the basket. "See, here a patch from that dress you loved—the one with yellow flowers. You love it so much you hated to grow out of it."

Neeny wrinkled her face like she taste something bad. "I don't know why I ever like a dress with bright, clashy colors like that, so loud they scream at you." She give a little shudder that send a chill in me, too. Like someone dump cold water on my head. "Anyway, I only wear store-bought dresses now," Neeny say.

"Oh," I say. Then I think of something.

"Come here, Neeny." I take her hand and lead her to my little garden behind the house. "See—Dada let me have my own garden now." I pick a big ripe tomato and hand it to Neeny. She scream so loud, Dada run out of the house thinkin' a snake bit her.

"What wrong with you, gal?"

"A worrrrrm! A big, squishy, green worrrrrm!" She drop my good tomato and run in the house.

Not the same Neeny, I think.

Neeny going tomorrow. Tonight we have a party for her. All the people come in their best clothes of bright, clashy colors. Neeny wear a dress the color of a new sky. The men gather under a big ol' live oak and tell tales.

The women lay out a long table with cucumbers and fried cabbage and pickled watermelon rind, shrimp, crab, and oysters. We hear the stories and laugh and laugh. Then we sing and dance. Neeny, too. Neeny have a good time, I think.

Neeny come like a visitor who didn't want to visit, but still I'm sad
she leavin'.

In the morning we stand at the riverbed and wait for Uncle Dink
to come with the fishing boat. Neeny put her arm around me and I
put my arm around her. She still my best cousin. I have a present for
her. I wrap it up in brown paper so she can't see it until she get home.

"Open it when you get home," I tell her. She promise me she will.

I give Neeny my new bed quilt so she can remember her family on the island. She can remember her best dress I know she still love, and my first party dress, and Aunt Carolina's wedding dress, Uncle Dink's old work shirt, and the curtains in Dada's bedroom. Neeny say they always remind her of a field of wildflowers.

"You come visit me, Essie. Make sure it's soon." I smile at Neeny. I don't know what she mean by soon. Soon to Dada mean when I get a lot bigger. I don't know what soon mean to me.

In the boat Neeny look back and wave. I wave back and think,
Neeny come—and now Neeny go.